COTTON FIELD SUNSET

LIFE RENEWED

LINDA GUCCIONE ALLARD

CONTENTS

ABBY RETURNS HOME

Chapter One

*A*bby Carpenter, burdened with a life-altering decision, found herself in her New York office for the last time. Her belongings were neatly packed, and she had bid her final farewells to friends and co-workers. The allure of the fast-paced, competitive world of New York had lost its charm. Her once ambitious plans for a corporate future no longer ignited her passion. Abby felt her heart had forgotten how to beat in the past few months. The changes within the Fairfield Design Associates of the New York company had dissolved her love for a career, and it was no longer a driving force in her life. She yearned for life with her family and the beloved cotton fields of West Texas and was filled with anticipation to live there again. The thought of reuniting with her family, feeling the familiar earth beneath her feet, and witnessing the cotton field sunsets once more filled her with a potent mix of bittersweet nostalgia and eager anticipation. Abby's life was about to change as she eagerly planned to return to her West Texas roots, a daunting and exhilarating decision filled with hope for a more fulfilling life.

Abby cast one final glance out the expansive window of her office, taking in the New York City skyline. She felt a profound sense of liberation from the chaos and stress that had hindered her from living a joyful and satisfying life. Today, she leaves the corporate world in her wake and embarks on a journey back to the cotton fields of West Texas, where life will become the pulse of her existence. The cotton farm, where she spent her childhood with her Aunt Lottie and Uncle Jack, was more than just a place; it was a sanctuary. It was like stepping into a detailed world crafted by God. There, she listened to the love songs of the birds: songs that felt like personal messages from God. Abby's mind was filled with visions of the cotton fields and God's plan for her in His world. Once again, she could hear God whispering in every moment of her existence, "You're mine, and I have great plans for you." She eagerly anticipated the beauty of the Desert Willow trees with their orchid-like blooms and the majestic elm trees that echoed in the wind, "Stand and take note of God passing by." Her deep connection to nature and spiritual beliefs brought her peace and contentment, a feeling she had yearned for in the corporate world.

⇛⇝

It was a beautiful evening as Abby stood on the balcony of her upstairs bedroom and witnessed the approach of nightfall over the farm. She revered the beauty that graced the cotton fields as she watched the magnificent sunset. It had been a long time since she was able to experience such a miraculous event. Abby cherished her beautiful memories of growing up on Uncle Jack and Aunt Lottie's cotton farm. Standing there gazing at the beauty of the cotton fields, thoughts of how much she missed living there flooded her mind. She had lived there since she was nine years old following the untimely deaths of her mother when she was seven and her father almost two years later. Abby was hard-pressed to remember feeling this happy in such a long time. She wondered if she had made the right choice, resigning from her executive position at a prominent New York firm to move back home to West Texas. She had an elegant lifestyle but an extremely stressful life in New York. She had lived there for over eight years after accepting a job with a well-known business firm. Abby was well respected by her peers and had, what she thought, a romantic relationship with Sherman Fairfield, the firm's CEO. After being back in West Texas for nearly two months, she realized how empty her life had been and no longer questioned her decision to leave New York. Abby was free of unmerited stress and felt she had renewed her life. She now had control of her life, and she loved it. Sure, she had a successful career, but what is being successful if you have no time for family or even the hope of having a family?

Abby stretched her arms towards the night sky and inhaled the fresh air. It felt delightful to welcome the fragrance of the cotton blossoms and witness the descent of evening. She gazed at the beauty of the cotton plants as they prepared for nightfall. In the morning, they would reach for the sky and grace the land with their greenery and unfolded cotton blossoms. Then, as though by magic, the blossoms would burst forth, leaving the fields adorned in white like newly fallen snow. Oh, how she missed the farm's beauty, freshness, and life.

Abby remembered how different life was for her in New York City. Instead of hearing a flock of geese fly overhead or farmers plowing their fields on their John Deere tractors, Abby's life consisted of noisy, over-crowded sidewalks, loud commuter buses, and skyscrapers that hid the sunrise and sunset. It was a concrete jungle where everyone raced to grab a cup of coffee and rushed to where they were going, struggling to arrive on time. Abby smiled at the thought and treasured her decision to leave this maze of corporate life and return to her first love of life---life in harmony with God's wonderful and beautiful world. For many, corporate life was the answer. But, for Abby, the cotton fields of West Texas had called her home.

Chapter Two

*A*bby's boss, Sherman Fairfield, the CEO of Fairfield Design Associates, finished packing the items from his office. He never realized how detailed and time-consuming moving one's possessions from one office to another could be. He was accustomed to Abby overseeing such projects. Even though she was the Manager of Corporate Events, Sherman never hesitated to request Abby's assistance with his responsibilities.

Following the company's merger, Sherman retained his position as CEO of the New York Facility, and his father, Hayden Fairfield, the company's owner, became the CEO of the newly expanded part of the company based in Los Angeles. Hayden Fairfield requested Abby's transfer to the Los Angeles facility as the Events Design General Manager. Her transfer and move would occur immediately following the holidays, which would not give her time to adjust to her new way of life or consider what might be most important to her. When Sherman related this information, Abby was distraught. She felt her relationship with Sherman did not mean as much to him as it did to her. It became evident that what controlled Sherman's business mind controlled his life. Sherman's dedication to the company outweighed his love for Abby, and now, Sherman realizes Abby has chosen a new life back in Texas.

As Sherman continued to pack his personal belongings, an elegantly framed picture of him and Abby tugged at his heart. There were many pictures of him and Abby attending special functions sponsored by the company. Each one reminded him of their close relationship as they worked together. Sherman thought about the day Abby left his office and his life. He remembered the heartbroken look on her face and the disbelief in his words. Sherman could not believe that Abby would give up her position in the company, especially when he considered her move to Los Angeles a considerable promotion. He took no thought as to how she would feel about leaving New York and moving to the West Coast. There had not been any previous discussion on the matter. Abby knew about the company's expansion plan but thought she and Sherman would surely stay and continue working together in New York. She could not imagine moving and working in the company without Sherman because Abby felt she and Sherman had a future together. She thought Sherman loved her and would be more in tune with her position in the company. Sherman hinted that she had been considered for a partnership. Now, she felt as though their relationship did not matter to Sherman. The only thing that mattered was her importance as an asset to the company.

Sherman could not understand how Abby could refuse such a prestigious position with the company after it had been a part of her life for over eight years. However, it was even more challenging to understand how Abby could walk out of his life: there were no future discussions and considerations as to how they might work out their differences. Abby was adamant about refusing the transfer to Los Angeles and incredibly optimistic about resigning from her present position. Sherman could not get his head around it. He could not understand how she could be so confident about what she wanted out of life.

Sherman carefully wrapped the framed pictures and placed them in the box. After packing his favorite photos and other treasured mementos, he developed a deep feeling of loneliness, which made him realize how much he missed Abby. He felt part of himself was missing and was unsure how to resolve the matter. He thought he had made a grave mistake by failing to tell Abby how much she meant to him. He did not believe that when she walked out of his office the day after Christmas, she was walking out of his life.

∾∾

"It's only six o'clock in the evening in Texas," Sherman mumbled. "I'm sure Abby won't mind if I call her." He grabbed his cell phone and pressed her number but immediately hung up. Something in his thoughts urged him to cancel the call. He was not sure of what he would say to her. He was not sure she would even talk to him or if she would even answer his call. It had been months since they had spoken to each other. It was not pleasant remembering their last encounter. Sherman was afraid of being rejected by her once again. Visions of their previous meeting before Abby left New York remained vivid in his memory. He recalled how disappointed he was when Abby refused the transfer to the Los Angeles office to become the General Manager of Corporate Events; not only had she refused the transfer and the promotion, but she had resigned from her position with the company and walked out of Sherman's office and out of his life.

Sherman took a deep breath and walked over to the couch in his office to sit down. He put his head in his hands and wept. He could not help but ask himself, "Why was I such a fool? I love her, but I let her walk out of my life. How could I do that? I do not know if or how I can get her back."

Chapter Three

The beautiful part of being back on the cotton farm with Aunt Lottie and Uncle Jack was being able to experience pleasurable and relaxing mornings. Abby missed this while she lived in New York. She was again thankful for fresh country air, coffee on the porch, and a morning walk down to the pasture to see Mollie, Uncle Jack's oldest and most cherished cow. Also, there was Old Shepp, Aunt Lottie's black and white German Shepherd/Sheepdog mix, who would trot along with them, bidding good morning to all the wildlife along the way. Abby remembers the day they got Old Shepp; they were told he was a one-of-a-kind German Shepherd/ Sheepdog puppy because he was the only one with black and white hair in the litter. It didn't matter to Aunt Lottie; she liked him the best among the litter and brought him home.

The smell of fresh, perked coffee summoned Abby to the kitchen this morning. "Good morning, Aunt Lottie," Abby said as she anxiously walked over to Aunt Lottie and hugged her.

"Where's Uncle Jack? Is he out taking a walk with Old Shepp already? I was hoping to go with him this morning. I wanted to check on Mollie's sore leg," Abby related to Aunt Lottie.

"I didn't know Mollie had a sore leg. When did this come about?" Aunt Lottie asked.

"Uncle Jack and I were checking out a broken plank in the gate of her pasture yesterday, and Mollie came over to greet us. She was limping. We didn't see any cuts or scratches, so we weren't too concerned, but we wanted to be sure and keep an eye on that leg," Abby replied.

"I bet that's where he took off after his first cup of coffee. He usually drinks an entire pot before starting his day." Aunt Lottie told Abby. "Old Shepp went with him." Aunt Lottie removed her apron and motioned to

Abby, "Come on, let's find them. I'm concerned. Uncle Jack never said a word about Mollie being hurt."

Abby and Aunt Lottie started walking down the road when they spied Old Shepp running up the road towards them and Uncle Jack leading Mollie by a rope into the barn.

"Jack, what's wrong with Mollie?" Aunt Lottie asked, walking into the barn behind them.

"Oh, somehow, she got a nail stuck in her left front hoof, and I needed to bring her into the barn to tie her up and remove it. The nail from the gate probably came out of the plank when she decided she'd nosey around. She must have stepped on the board, and the nail was sticking up just enough to get caught in her hoof. I don't think it will be a problem to remove it. It doesn't look as though it penetrated her flesh. It just seems it made it uncomfortable when she walked," Jack explained. "Abby and I noticed her limping yesterday, but she took off from us and headed toward the other side of the meadow. You know Mollie, she doesn't like you to tamper with her. She's been limping quite a bit on that leg lately, though. I need Doc Collins to look at it. I'll give him a call."

"Okay. When you finish with her, come in and call Doc Collins, and then have pancakes with Abby and me," Aunt Lottie told Jack. Aunt Lottie always enjoyed the family being together for breakfast, and Abby looked forward to this time before getting into the day's events.

Chapter Four

Immediately following breakfast, Abby called Mayor Stewart to set up an appointment to finalize the establishment of her Events Design Business in Gail, a small town established southwest of Aunt Lottie and Uncle Jack's cotton farm. She was excited about the adventure and anxious to get it rolling. Abby felt having her own business in the nearby town close to Aunt Lottie and Uncle Jack was a blessing in disguise.

❧❦

"Good morning. You've reached Mayor Stewart's Office. How may I help you?" Gloria Foster, Mayor Stewart's secretary, asked when she answered the phone in the courthouse.

"Good morning, Gloria. This is Abby Carpenter. I need to make an appointment with Mayor Stewart. Will he be available sometime today?" Abby asked.

"Abby, he was expecting to hear from you today. Let me transfer your call," Gloria replied.

"Good morning, Abby," Mayor Stewart politely answered. I was just about to call you to see if we could meet for lunch today." Mayor Stewart said.

"That sounds good to me, Mayor Stewart," Abby answered with a tone of excitement.

"Great! How about twelve thirty at Murphy's Beef Shack? Does that work for you?" Mayor Stewart asked Abby.

"Yes, Sir. I will see you then." Abby answered.

After finishing her call with Mayor Stewart, Abby returned to the kitchen to help with dishes and share the news of a lunch meeting with Mayor Stewart. She invited Aunt Lottie to come with her, but Aunt

Lottie said she needed to stay home with Uncle Jack because Doc Collins was stopping by around one o'clock to check on Mollie.

"Couldn't Uncle Jack get the nail out of her hoof?" Abby asked.

"That wasn't a problem," Aunt Lottie replied. "Uncle Jack thinks she could have hurt herself, butting up against the gate to get out and go to the barn. He said she still acts frightened when she feels a storm heading our way. Mollie is his prized cow, having given birth to five calves. I believe he loves that cow more than me, sometimes. And Mollie loves him."

❧

Following lunch with Mayor Stewart, Abby rushed back to Aunt Lottie and Uncle Jack's to share the news of the business deal she finalized with the mayor. She wondered if Doc Collins would still be there because she wanted to see him and talk to him about Mollie.

When she arrived at the house, Aunt Lottie was in the kitchen, and Uncle Jack and Doc Collins were on the porch having a glass of iced tea.

"Hi, Doc," Abby said in her friendly way, walking over to hug him. It's so good to see you. It's been a long time. I fondly remember you taking care of Old Shepp and Mollie."

"It's good to see you also, Abby. It has been a long time. You have grown into a beautiful young lady." Doc Collins replied. "Your uncle tells me you've given up on corporate life in New York and have moved back to Texas."

"That's right," Abby answered. "I finally realized corporate life was not for me anymore. I missed the beauty of West Texas and my loving family."

"I am so pleased to hear that, and I know a lot of people have missed you," Doc Collins told Abby.

"I'm delighted to be back in Texas with Aunt Lottie and Uncle Jack. I've been away for too long." Abby replied to Doc Collins, then turned to

Uncle Jack and asked him about Mollie. "So, what's wrong with Mollie? Was there a problem getting the nail out?"

"No, it looks like she hurt her leg while trying to escape the pasture. It seems she doesn't want to stay in her pasture as long as we feel she should."

Having answered all their questions about Mollie, Doc Collins graciously said goodbye, climbed into his pickup, and waved as he drove down the road.

☙❧

Uncle Jack and Aunt Lottie could hardly wait to ask Abby about her visit with Mayor Stewart. "Abby, how was your visit with Mayor Stewart? Were you able to get it all worked out?"

"Oh, yes," Abby answered. "He and his wife have an old house they inherited from his grandmother, and they want to renovate it and let me use it for my place of business. They love the idea of having an Event Design business in Gail. They approve of my ideas for the business and are anxious to start the renovation immediately. I am so excited."

"Where is the house located?" Uncle Jack asked.

"It's on the street right behind the courthouse," Abby answered. "You can see it from Mayor Stewart's office. Also, Mayor Stewart wants me to design the renovation, but he will handle all the financial details. I will rent the house from him, which sounds wonderful."

FAMILY CHANGES

Chapter One

Life changed rapidly for Aunt Lottie and Uncle Jack when Abby moved back to Texas. They were happy that Abby was living with them and enjoyed the energy she brought into their lives. Abby was respectful of their age and tried to be as helpful as they would allow. She tried not to interfere with their plans, and they understood her goal to establish her business.

Mayor Stewart managed the renovations of his grandmother's house, which went smoothly as expected and were completed ahead of schedule. Abby stayed busy taking care of the events being scheduled locally. Her calendar filled up fast. People as far east as Abilene and as far north as Lubbock scheduled Abby to plan and orchestrate their special event. Abby was happy and grateful to be part of her West Texas heritage again and delighted in the success of her business.

Every morning, upon waking, she eagerly faced the new day. There was no longer any humdrum about what to expect for the day's plans. Each day was a new adventure—a happy adventure. Abby was a people person who delighted in making new friends and reacquainting herself with old friends.

"What a beautiful morning, "Abby announced as she bounced down the steps into the kitchen. She could smell the delicious cinnamon apple muffins baking that Aunt Lottie always made when she was growing up. It was a special treat for Abby and her brother, Gordon when Aunt Lottie would make muffins for them in the morning. Even Old Shepp got to have a muffin, which made his day.

"Good morning to you, Abby," Aunt Lottie replied lovingly. I'm glad to see you so happy and full of energy. The muffins are ready if you would like to have one now."

"Yes, ma'am. Thanks," Abby said as she reached to grab one. "Where's Uncle Jack? Is he checking on Mollie?"

"Yes, he could hardly wait to finish his coffee before going to the barn and walking her down to the pasture. He doesn't want to leave her out during the night but wants her to have a full day in the pasture to graze and soak up the sunshine," Aunt Lottie replied with a deep concern for her husband and Mollie. "Uncle Jack said he heard the weather report early this morning, and the prediction is that heavy rain and high winds may occur this afternoon. He suggests that if you have any errands, do them this morning because this could be a bad storm."

Abby poured herself another cup of coffee, grabbed another muffin, and headed out the door to check on Uncle Jack and Mollie. She wanted to catch them before they reached the pasture so she could check Mollie's leg and hoof. She was concerned and knew it was very upsetting to Uncle Jack to see Mollie injured.

Seeing them on the road not too far ahead, Abby yelled as loud as she could, "Hey, Uncle Jack. Wait up!" She started running towards them, hoping to catch up before they reached the gate to the pasture.

Uncle Jack turned, waved, and slowed down. Abby caught up with them just before they reached the pasture, and when Uncle Jack tried to walk Mollie through the gate, she refused to go in and began tugging on the rope to escape. It took most of Uncle Jack's strength to keep her from breaking loose and starting to head back toward the barn.

The wind had picked up, and then Abby began to feel raindrops. "I thought the wind and rain wasn't due until this afternoon," Abby remarked to Uncle Jack as they began to walk faster and faster towards the barn. "I guess Mollie knows more about the weather than the weatherman."

The storm's intensity had increased from the first report earlier that morning to the latest report. Aunt Lottie stood on the back porch, hoping to see Uncle Jack, Abby, and Mollie walking down the roadway heading for the barn. She was concerned for their safety and prayed they would make it in time before the full brunt of the storm hit.

Aunt Lottie watched the road for any sign of them, and when she began to hear voices, she was relieved to see Mollie, Uncle Jack, and Abby make it into the barn just before the wind grew more robust and the rain began to pour down.

Uncle Jack put Mollie into her stall and secured the gate while Abby closed the large barn doors and checked the smaller door, which was rattling quite a bit.

Hearing the rain pound the barn's roof, they decided to wait until it slowed down before going to the house. Suddenly, the smaller barn door flew open. The wind caught it, tore it off its hinges, and sent it sailing across the yard, just missing the back porch steps before it landed in the vegetable garden.

Aunt Lottie heard the commotion, saw the door fly past the porch steps, and then breathed a sigh of relief, seeing that it wasn't something more serious. She knew as soon as the rain ceased to pellet the ground, Uncle Jack and Abby would make their way to the house.

After the storm subsided, Uncle Jack and Abby walked to the house, leaving Mollie in the barn. Aunt Lottie had lunch prepared, and when they finished eating, they went outside to check for damage. They looked for the small barn door and found it lying upside down near the side of the vegetable garden. Uncle Jack felt sure he could replace the hinges and secure it again.

Chapter Two

*G*randpa Cliff often drove the red tractor to the family cemetery near the far west edge of the cotton farm every chance he could. This morning, he was up very early, looking forward to completing his planned work in the family's graveyard. He told Lottie and Jack that he would be going early and would plan to be back before any storms hit the area that afternoon.

As soon as Grandpa Cliff arrived at the cemetery, he unpacked his tools and got to work on his plans for the day. He did take notice of the dark sky in the far northwest distance but paid no mind since it was bright and sunny at the cemetery. He planned to cultivate the flowers and remove the weeds around the graves. He loved spending time at the family graveyard and sometimes sat on the wooden bench beneath the canopy of desert willow trees. It was beautiful and peaceful there, and a slight breeze would always blow, giving a soothing effect. He couldn't help but reminisce about his loved ones who were no longer in his life. He was able to grasp the feeling of being with them again. His loving family included his parents, Clifton and Martha Sanders, and his wife, Hannah Rowe Sanders, and buried next to Hannah was their firstborn, Jeffery Cliff Sanders, who was only two years old at the time of his death.

Not realizing how much time had passed, Grandpa Cliff stopped what he was doing and checked his pocket watch. It was almost five o'clock, so he knew he needed to head home because Lottie would have supper ready by six. He loaded his tools, climbed onto the tractor, and sat for a few minutes to gaze over the cemetery and soak up the ambiance before starting the motor.

"Now what?" Grandpa Cliff thought to himself when he turned the key, and the tractor wouldn't start. "Wouldn't you know it? I don't have my phone with me either. I guess I'll have to start walking towards Hamilton Automotive in Gail, which is much closer than the house. I can call Jack and Lottie from there."

⧫

Jack finished repairing the barn door just in time to go to the house and clean up for dinner. He looked around the yard and down the road, hoping to see Grandpa Cliff before entering the house. He thought Grandpa Cliff should surely be back by now.

"Have you seen or heard from my dad?" Jack asked Lottie upon entering the kitchen. "He doesn't seem to be back from the cemetery yet. I hope he's not having trouble getting that old tractor started. I told him it needed a new battery, but you know my dad. He loves that old tractor, and though he takes good care of it, it is still an old tractor. He may have gone to Gail to get a battery and then the cemetery, which would make him get a late start on his project."

"Uncle Jack, would you like me to call the auto store and check on him for you?" Abby asked.

"Sure, you do that, and I'll watch from the porch in case I hear him coming down the road," Jack replied.

Abby immediately called the auto store, hoping Grandpa Cliff would be there, but they said they hadn't seen him that day. Aunt Lottie knew that dinner would have to wait when she saw Uncle Jack and Abby get in Jack's pick-up and head towards the family cemetery.

When they got to the graveyard, they saw the red tractor parked under some trees, but there was no sign of Grandpa Cliff. Jack climbed in the red tractor and tried to start it. He tried jumping it with the cables he had in the pickup, but no luck. Yep, he was right. The battery was dead. They looked all around the area but didn't see any signs of

Grandpa Cliff, so they figured he must be walking to the auto store to use their phone to call Jack and Lottie, or even Abby, for that matter. He was stranded.

Uncle Jack decided to drive down the road from the cemetery to Gail in case Grandpa Cliff was walking to the auto store several miles away, where he knew he could get help.

"Uncle Jack, look! That looks like Grandpa Cliff walking on the side of the road?" Abby said excitedly. "I believe it is," Jack said, slowing down and moving closer to the shoulder of the road. Jack could see that it was his dad.

Abby rolled down her window, yelling and waving her arm, hoping to get his attention. When Grandpa Cliff heard the yelling, he turned to see who it was and felt relieved to see Jack and Abby.

Jack pulled over, stopped his pickup, and Abby jumped out and hugged Grandpa Cliff. "We were really worried about you, Grandpa."

Grandpa Cliff climbed into the pickup, gave Jack a sheepish look, and said, "I know, I know. I couldn't get the tractor started. Thanks for coming to rescue me."

Jack proceeded silently to the auto store, where they could get a battery before heading home. He wasn't about to lecture his dad. He was relieved they found him safe and sound and thankful they would be together for dinner. Tomorrow was another day. The tractor would get a new battery. All would be fine.

Chapter Three

*U*ncle Jack and Grandpa Cliff walked into Hamilton's Automotive to pick up the battery for the red tractor. Harold Hamilton, the owner, had to order it from the supplier in Abilene and called Uncle Jack the next day to tell him the battery had arrived and was ready for pickup.

"Good morning, Jack," Harold said, greeting him pleasantly. I'm sorry we didn't have one in stock last night when you stopped by. That's an odd-sized battery; we don't keep them in stock. We don't have many calls for them around here. You have an ancient tractor."

"Yep, I sure do," Grandpa Cliff spoke up with a chuckle. "It is the first tractor I ever owned, and it is my pride and joy. I know it's old because I am old, so we fit together quite nicely. I bought that tractor shortly after I got married long ago. I was raising cotton on my dad's 300 acres, and when the adjacent farm went up for sale, my wife and I purchased it. It had a small house and barn, and I've lived there with my red tractor ever since." Everyone smiled and chuckled at his remarks.

Harold's son, Josh, brought the battery from the store's back room. "Shall I put this in the truck for you, Mr. Carpenter?" Josh asked.

"Yes, thank you," Jack graciously answered. "Hey, I recognize you. You're Josh, right?" Uncle Jack asked when he recognized him. "You and Abby dated when you were in college, right?"

Josh nodded his head as if to say yes and smiled.

"I haven't seen you around these parts in a long time. Where have you been?" Jack asked.

"I've been working for my friend, Jeremy Sikes, who lives in Floyd County. He needed help managing his mother's 300-acre cotton farm after his dad, David, suffered a stroke." Josh related to Jack. "Jeremy's twin brothers were in college at Louisiana Tech on football scholarships and couldn't leave school to help because they would lose their scholarships. They have both graduated and plan to work with their dad to manage the farm. So, I wanted to move back here, work in my dad's cotton fields, and help in the store on weekends.

"By the way, did you know Abby has moved back to Texas?" Uncle Jack commented. "She gave up her corporate life in New York and is living with Lottie and me for now."

"Really?" Josh said, surprised. "We used to keep in touch, but I haven't heard from her in several years. So, what is she going to do here? Does she plan on staying here?"

"She has established her own business and is using her expertise. She is an Event Design Planner. That's what she did for this large architectural firm in New York. Mayor Stewart is so impressed with her plans to establish her business here in Gail that he plans to renovate his grandmother's old house, the one behind the Courthouse, and let her use it as her business office," Uncle Jack related to Josh. "I'm surprised you haven't run into each other. She's been here almost two months now."

"I guess we just don't travel on the same paths," Josh remarked. He was thinking how great it was to know that she was here and that there was a possibility that he could see her again.

"Hey, why don't you come by sometime to say hello?" Uncle Jack offered, sporting a big grin. "I know she'd love to see you."

"Thanks, Mr. Carpenter, I'd like to do that," Josh said, smiling back.

Uncle Jack and Aunt Lottie always had a soft spot for Josh. They felt Josh and Abby would make a lovely couple, but Abby's head turned from thinking about a future with Josh when a New York firm grabbed her expertise and hired her immediately. He remembered how broken-hearted they were when Abby accepted the position in New York, but they didn't want to hold her back from a good opportunity. They tried to understand her decision and graciously supported her.

Chapter Four

*B*irthdays were always special celebrations, and Abby looked forward to Aunt Lottie's upcoming birthday in October to be no different. Abby first called Gordon to share her idea about the party with him. Then she called Jenny Pearl and discussed the plans for the surprise birthday party for her mom, who would celebrate her 50th birthday next month. Abby hoped Jenny Pearl and her family could attend since they lived in Los Alamos, New Mexico. Due to the top security of his work, Chad, Jenny's husband, had a demanding work schedule, and Abby knew they would need to make plans early.

"What a wonderful surprise for my mom," Jenny told Abby. "I'll let Chad know now so we can plan to be there. It will be another great time to be together. I'm excited about this."

Abby had always cherished memories of the surprise birthday party Aunt Lottie and Uncle Jack gave her and Gordon after their mother and father died. She always felt blessed when she recalled the party and how it was the critical point when she and Gordon began to feel their lives come together. Anytime Abby celebrates a birthday, she returns to that special day she will remember forever.

It happened years ago, following the tragic death of Abby and Gordon's mother and then the unexpected death of their father a little over a year later; Abby and Gordon didn't have their last birthdays celebrated. They often mentioned how they missed having a birthday party several times to Aunt Lottie, so she and Uncle Jack wondered how they could make it up to them.

Aunt Lottie and Uncle Jack decided to plan a surprise party at Murphy's and invite all their friends and families to the celebration. Everyone needed to be at Murphy's before Aunt Lottie and Uncle Jack arrived with Abby, Gordon, and their baby girl, Jenny Pearl. Everyone needed to be seated to watch as Aunt Lottie and Uncle Jack walked Abby and Gordon to their table. Aunt Lottie held their hands, and Uncle Jack followed behind, carrying Jenny Pearl.

It was an unforgettable evening for the children, considering it hadn't been long since they had come to live with their aunt and uncle.

As Abby walked towards their table, she noticed it was all decorated with balloons and streamers. Abby asked Aunt Lottie who was having a party. When they reached their reserved table, everyone stood up and clapped. Aunt Lottie and Uncle Jack lifted Abby and Gordon, stood them on a chair, and put birthday hats on them. Then the waitress brought a beautiful birthday cake and set it in the middle of the table. She lit nine candles on one side for Abby and four candles for Gordon on the other. Everyone sang Happy Birthday, and Aunt Lottie and Uncle Jack were tearful as they watched the smiles appear on their little faces. They couldn't help but have tears of joy for them. It was an evening filled with great happiness they would never forget.

Chapter Five

*W*hen Aunt Lottie entered the kitchen the morning of her birthday, she thought only of putting on a pot of coffee and starting breakfast. However, she was surprised to see a beautiful bouquet of roses on the kitchen table. She thought they must be from Jack but was quite surprised when she read the card.

> *Happy Birthday, Aunt Lottie.*
> *Thank you for loving us all these years.*
> *We can never thank you enough for caring.*
> *We love you,*
>
> *- Abby and Gordon*

Aunt Lottie didn't notice when Abby entered the kitchen. Abby walked up behind her, hugged her, and said, "You are the most important person in my life. I love you for loving me and for loving Gordon. You brought peace and happiness into our lives when we felt we had no one to love us. You loved us and cared for us when our mother died, and we were left with no hope of having a mother again."

Abby squeezed Aunt Lottie tighter, and the tears streamed down their cheeks. This would be an extraordinary day for Aunt Lottie and her family.

Abby walked over to the coffee pot and poured a cup for Aunt Lottie and herself. They both went to the back porch to sit and enjoy the autumn breezes. It was a beautiful morning, and Jack and Old Shepp were coming down the road, returning from their morning walk to take Mollie to the pasture. Old Shepp was a faithful dog and watched over

Uncle Jack, Aunt Lottie, and Grandpa Cliff. It wasn't morning unless Old Shepp got to walk with them and take Mollie to the pasture.

When Old Shepp ran up to the porch to greet Aunt Lottie and Abby, he always got excited to see them and greeted them lovingly. Uncle Jack was close behind and walked over to Aunt Lottie. "I love you, and happy birthday, Sweetheart," Jack said as he bent over and kissed her. May you be blessed today with the wishes of your heart."

"Thank you, Jack. I feel blessed to be spending my birthday with you, Abby, and Grandpa Cliff," Aunt Lottie replied. She had no idea what the rest of the day would bring.

❧☙

Gordon, Robyn, and Cornell arrived at Murphy's Beef Shack forty-five minutes before Uncle Jack and Aunt Lottie arrived for her birthday dinner. Uncle Jack planned to have Aunt Lottie there by six o'clock. A particular room had been reserved and decorated in the back for the surprise celebration. Abby was in charge and felt a sense of pride doing this for Aunt Lottie.

Gordon stayed in touch with Jenny Pearl and Chad and watched for their arrival. They assured Gordon they would arrive before Uncle Jack arrived with Aunt Lottie. Even Grandpa Cliff and his date were there early, along with Mayor Stewart and his wife, Lizzie, and other close friends.

"Wow, Jack, it looks like Murphy's is crowded tonight. It's a good thing you made reservations, huh?" Aunt Lottie said as she surveyed the parking lot.

When they entered the restaurant, Jack told the maître d they had reservations for two in the special events room. They were then led to the reserved room, where everyone was anticipating Aunt Lottie's arrival. When she walked through the door, everyone stood up, applauded, and began to sing, "Happy Birthday to you." It was a memorable evening for Aunt Lottie and her family and close friends.

After dinner, the family gathered at Aunt Lottie's and Uncle Jack's for a nightcap. While everyone was gathered in the living room, Chad made a toast to Aunt Lottie, expressing the family's love for her, and then Jenny Pearl made a special announcement. She stood up, faced her mom and dad, and lovingly said, "I wish to announce that Emily Jean is going to have a little sister or brother in May."

Chapter Six

*A*bby was awakened by the chattering of Emily Jean and Cornell's small voices talking with Aunt Lottie in the kitchen. Cornell couldn't help but giggle as he listened to Emily Jean calling Aunt Lottie Lolly.

"Aunt Lottie, why does Emily Jean call you 'Lolly' and not 'Aunt Lottie'?" Cornell asked.

"Well, because I am her grandma and not her aunt." Aunt Lottie hoped her answer would suffice, but it made for more questions.

"What do you mean you're not her aunt but her grandma?" Cornell said with a puzzled look on his face.

"Cornell, do you remember when I told you the story of your grandma, Pearl?" Aunt Lottie began to try and explain.

"Yes, Ma'am," Cornell politely answered. "She died when my daddy was just a small boy, right? And she is my Grandma Pearl. I wish I knew her and could see her."

"Yes, Pearl is your grandma. I am Emily Jean's grandma," Aunt Lottie said, hoping he would understand. "Your daddy's mother was Pearl, my sister, which made me your daddy's Aunt Lottie. When your daddy and his sister, Abby, who you call Auntie Abbs, came to live with us after their mother died, they called me Aunt Lottie. That was my name to them."

"But Emily Jean calls you Lolly. Why?" Cornell asked, trying to figure it out.

He still didn't quite understand, so Aunt Lottie tried to explain it further. The more she tried to explain, the more confused Cornell seemed. Finally, he put his head in his hands and asked, "Can I call you Lolly, too?"

Aunt Lottie leaned over and gave Cornell a big hug. With a tear or two in her eyes, she told him, "That would be wonderful. I would love for you to call me 'Lolly.'"

Filled with excitement, Cornnell jumped off his chair and ran to tell his mom and dad that Aunt Lottie would also be his 'Lolly.'

Aunt Lottie, Uncle Jack, and Emily Jean stood on the back porch, along with Jenny Pearl, Chad, and Abby, waving goodbye. They watched Gordon, Robyn, and Cornell drive off, headed for home. Gordon and Robyn wanted to stay for the entire weekend with the family but couldn't because Gordon had some work-related duties that needed to be completed before Monday.

"Dad," Cornell yelled from the backseat, "isn't it great that Aunt Lottie is now my 'Lolly,' too? Isn't that just great? That's like being a grandma, like Grandma Pearl, but I get to see her and hug her. Right, Dad?"

Gathering his emotions before answering, Gordon told his sweet son, "That's right, Cornell. You have two grandmas now." Robyn looked over at Gordon and smiled. She felt blessed to witness such love between Gordon and his family.

❧⚜

Abby helped Aunt Lottie clean the kitchen while Jenny Pearl and Chad took Emily Jean on a walk to see Mollie in her pasture.

"What a great and wonderful celebration," Chad remarked to Jenny as they walked. "It was so perfect how you also announced our second child's coming. That was great thinking, Jenny."

"My mom was overwhelmed, wasn't she?" Jenny replied. "We are so blessed, Chad. You see, several doctors told my mom she would never have children. And then, it happened. It was nothing short of a miracle. My mom's older sister, Pearl, was the first one, besides my dad, of course, with whom my mom shared the news of her pregnancy."

"I never knew about that," Chad remarked. "So, that's why Pearl, your Aunt Pearl, was so anxious to visit your mom. That's when the terrible accident happened, and she died, right?"

"Yes, Jenny Pearl answered. "That's why I'm named after her. My mom felt guilty for so long because she wanted Pearl to see where they lived, help her set up a nursery, and share the joy with her. They were very close sisters even though Pearl was ten years older."

"So, Abby and Gordon are like siblings to you, aren't they?" Chad said, realizing that Lottie and Jack raised them like their children. "Jenny, you are so blessed with a wonderful family, and I am blessed to be in your life."

ABBY'S FUTURE

Chapter One

*A*bby met with Mayor Stewart and his wife to discuss their 50th wedding anniversary celebration. He and Lizzie had great plans and discussed the location, decorations, and menu with Abby in grave detail. They showed her pictures of their wedding and wedding reception so Abby could visualize what they discussed.

"I think what your thoughts are, Mayor Stewart, is that you and Mrs. Stewart want it to be as close to the theme of your wedding as possible," Abby said. "That will not be a problem. I didn't realize you married in your grandmother's house, though. Of course, how would I know that? I wasn't born yet," Abby said with a chuckle. "I'm so happy the parlor and the ballroom were left in their original condition when we renovated."

"So am I," Mayor Stewart added. "I didn't know what Lizzie was planning, but that's great."

"What is the date? That's extremely important," Abby commented. "Will the date fall on a weekend, I hope? Weekends always work better for the attendees."

"Yep, it works out that way this year; it's on a Sunday, the first Sunday in December. We'd like to have it around 5:00 or 6:00 in the evening. Just think, Abby, you won't have to come from New York. I'm beyond happy for you, us, and the town of Gail."

Abby gathered her notes and the wedding pictures Mayor Stewart and Lizzie had given her and put them in her briefcase. "I'm going to make some calls and get the ball rolling on securing decorations, getting samples for the invitations, and ordering plates, napkins, and cups to get exactly what Lizzie wants. Don't forget to work on the menu, and I'll be in my office if you need me."

When Abby left the mayor's office, she went to her office and made her phone calls before she headed home for lunch. Not only was Abby setting up the Stewart's 50th wedding anniversary celebration in December, but she was also in charge of the Annual Christmas Bazaar and Dance, held at the Community Center Barn and was always scheduled for the third Saturday in December. She would not be starting the decorations from scratch this year, though. Uncle Jack and the Community Center's committee stored last year's decorations in the storage area of the Community Center Barn. So, all that Abby needed to do was check on her pre-order of the fresh Christmas trees that lined the walkway, the 20 ft. Douglas fir and the poinsettia plants. This could be handled with one phone call. After the arrival of the trees, Abby needed to set up the decorating schedule. The Annual Christmas Bazaar and Dance was on everybody's calendar, and Abby would be in Texas to enjoy all the festivities.

☙❧

"Time seems to fly here," Abby thought as she drove back to the house to have lunch with Aunt Lottie and Uncle Jack. "It's already lunchtime, and I just started working on today's plans."

When Abby drove up, she saw a bright blue pickup parked in front of the house. Who could that be? she thought. I've never seen that truck here before. But, after all, Uncle Jack and Aunt Lottie know a lot of people.

When Abby reached the porch, she heard laughter and familiar voices. Her heart started beating faster when she thought she recognized the voice of Josh Hamilton, whom she dated in college but hadn't seen in several years. What would he be doing here, she thought. Surely, Aunt Lottie and Uncle Jack didn't invite him to visit. Uncle Jack never mentioned having a connection with him anymore. The last thing Abby heard about Josh was he moved to Floyd County to manage a cotton farm with a friend. And that was several years ago. She hadn't been in touch with Josh since their break-up after his visit to New York to celebrate her 25th birthday.

Abby felt anxious and nervous thinking of the possibility of seeing him again. Her palms began to sweat, and she felt her heart about to beat out of her chest. She wasn't sure how to handle this encounter. Their last meeting wasn't one of her best memories of their relationship.

❧

Josh did all he could to contain his excitement as the plane entered the gate. He knew Abby would be waiting for him in the terminal, and he was anxious to see her. It had been nearly a year since they had spent time together. Abby invited Josh to come to New York to celebrate her 25th birthday. Though months apart, they were able to keep their relationship alive. Lately, Abby felt the distance between them had become a challenge, and Abby felt Josh needed to decide.

Josh hugged and kissed Abby immediately when he got into the terminal. He took her hand in his, and they talked nonstop as they walked to her car. She couldn't believe the intensity of the loving emotions that ignited within her when she saw him and felt his arms around her. Abby missed his presence in her life and was afraid their relationship would change drastically if they didn't discuss their future direction.

Abby drove Josh to the hotel where he stayed during his visit to New York. "I know you will be comfortable here," Abby told him. "I'm sorry to drop you off so soon, but I must finish a few things at my office before taking off the next few days. I'll return around six to pick you up for the party. Josh, it's so good to have you here. I've missed you. Thanks for coming." Abby smiled and leaned over to kiss Josh before he got out of the car. As she drove off, she blew him another kiss.

As promised, Abby picked Josh up around six and headed to her 25th birthday party. The room was lavishly decorated with balloons and streamers, an elegant buffet was served, and a band played their favorite music. The evening, with Josh there, was everything Abby had hoped.

Abby introduced Josh to her co-workers, especially her boss, Sherman Fairfield. Josh was happy to be with Abby and to meet her friends, but in his heart, he knew Abby's goals in life had drastically changed.

After they danced to one of their memorable songs, they sat at their table to discuss their future. Josh reached across the table, took Abby's hand in his, and said, "Abby, I love you, and I want more than anything for us to continue our relationship, but Abby, I can't move to New York, nor can I ask you to give up everything you have worked so hard for here."

Josh knew his love for Abby would always remain in his heart, but he felt there wasn't any way their lives could mesh. She lived in a corporate world, which Josh knew he could not fit into.

❧

Abby quietly opened the kitchen door and walked to the living room. She was correct; the voice she heard earlier was Josh, who had stopped by to visit Aunt Lottie and Uncle Jack in hopes of seeing Abby. His eyes gleamed when Josh saw her in all her beauty, and he was at a loss for words.

"Josh, it's good to see you," Abby said, breaking the silence. Then Uncle Jack broke into the conversation by telling Abby that he ran into Josh at Hamilton Automotive, which Josh's father owned, and had invited him to come by and visit sometime.

"Your uncle tells me you have moved back to Texas," Josh said, entering the conversation.

"That's true," Abby said as she walked over and sat by Aunt Lottie on the couch. I realized how much I missed my family and West Texas," she replied without taking her eyes off Josh for one minute. "So, what have you been doing these past few years?"

"I've been working in Floyd County helping a friend manage his parents' cotton farm. Do you remember Jeremy Sikes?"

Abby gave Josh a puzzled look. She wasn't sure she remembered but didn't admit it.

"Well, his dad suffered a stroke several years ago, and I was able to help. I didn't know they would need me to assist Jeremy until his dad finished physical therapy and could handle the equipment again," Josh related to Abby. "Listen, I need to go. My dad has a list of errands for me to run," Josh said as he stood up to leave. "It's been great visiting with you all.

Josh began walking towards the door when Aunt Lottie and Abby stood up. Aunt Lottie turned to Josh and said, "Next time, plan to stay and have lunch with us."

"Thank you," Josh replied. "I will, thank you." Josh turned to Abby and said, "It was good to see you, Abby. I'm glad you're back in Texas."

Abby smiled, looked into Josh's eyes, and said, "There's no other place I'd rather be."

Abby watched Josh climb into his truck. She waved goodbye from the porch and watched as he drove away. Thoughts of the days spent in college with Josh made Abby realize how much she missed being with him. Her mind drifted to the happiness they shared while dating in college. She never thought their lives would take them in separate directions after graduation.

After Aunt Lottie, Uncle Jack, and Abby finished having lunch together, Abby politely excused herself and told them she had an appointment in Gail at 2:00 and needed to leave.

When Uncle Jack noticed the time, he remembered they were supposed to meet with Gordon later that afternoon in Lubbock. Lottie suggested they take Emily's cradle to Ben Sawyer, Jack's friend, who lives in Post, to repair it. Ben owns and operates a carpentry shop, and he made this beautiful cradle for Lottie and Jack when they were expecting their first baby. So, when Jack noticed one of the runners on the cradle had cracked, Jack called Ben immediately because he needed to make sure Ben would have time to repair it before the Christmas rush. Jack knew Ben would get extremely busy before Christmas with orders.

"Hey, Ben. This is Jack," Jack announced when Ben answered his phone.

"Jack, ole buddy," Ben replied. "It's good to hear from you. How's everything going?"

"Good. We're good. Say, do you remember that cradle you made for us when we were expecting Jenny? Well, it needs repair. Our little granddaughter, Emily Jean, loves sleeping in that cradle, and they'll be here again this year for the Christmas holidays. So, I was hoping you could get it repaired by then. Also, Lottie and I are expecting another grandchild in May. We're going to need that cradle."

"Wow, another grandchild. Congratulations! Your family keeps growing." Ben remarked. "I'll make it look like knew. When would you like to bring it to me?"

"I was hoping today. Is that alright?" Jack asked. "Lottie and I need to go to Lubbock to see Gordon about some legal stuff, and we thought we could drop by your place on the way home."

"Great! About what time can I expect you?" Ben asked. "Hey, why don't you meet us at The Burger Stop, and we'll eat and visit?"

"That sounds great. Around six?" Jack asked.

"Great. See you then, my friend. Don't forget the cradle," Ben said with a chuckle.

ȘȘ

When Aunt Lottie and Uncle Jack arrived at Gordon's Law Offices, his secretary greeted them and showed them to his private office.

Gordon, as always, greeted them respectfully with love and hugs and told them how glad he was to see them.

"I'm glad you could come today so we could sign and get these papers notarized," Gordon told Uncle Jack. "I've looked over everything, and the bottom line is that the oil company wants to extend the lease from two years to five years. Also, they are offering you more per barrel of oil. It's not much more per barrel, but it's significant considering the extended lease and the monthly price increase."

Jack and Lottie signed the papers and completed the transactions. As they were about to leave, Robyn and Cornell showed up. Robyn had just picked Cornell up from school.

"Well, look who's here," Uncle Jack remarked, looking at Cornell and ruffling his hair. "Glad we were still here to see you before leaving."

"Hi, Uncle Jack and Lolly," Cornell yelled as he ran over to hug them. "Are you coming to my house?" Cornell asked immediately.

"No, we were just headed on our way home. We plan to eat at the Burger Stop in Post and meet some friends. Would you like to come with us, Cornell, and spend the weekend?" Uncle Jack asked, glancing over at Gordon and Robyn. "I could sure use some help tomorrow."

"Can I go with them?" Cornell pleaded with his parents. He put his hands together in a praying position and continued to beg, "Please, please, please."

Chapter Two

*C*ornell was always a joy, bringing bittersweet memories to Uncle Jack. He couldn't resist that little boy's pleading and wanting to help. Cornell loved riding the red tractor with Uncle Jack and Grandpa Cliff, for that matter, whenever he could, especially when Grandpa Cliff allowed him to steer it.

∽∾

"Lottie, Gordon is going to ride with me in the fields today," Jack told Lottie as he and Gordon walked to the barn to get the red tractor. "I want to teach him how to plow the fields to plant the cotton."

"Jack, be very careful. He's only five years old and can hardly see over the steering wheel," Lottie reminded Jack.

"I know, but he's my buddy. We work together." Jack yelled back at Lottie before going into the barn.

"Come on, Gordon, climb up here and hold on tight, Uncle Jack told him as he pulled Gordon up and squeezed him into the seat. Uncle Jack started the engine and let Gordon help him steer the tractor down the road beside the cotton fields. This was Gordon's first time steering the tractor into the cotton fields and helping Uncle Jack plow.

The wind blew Gordon's sandy brown hair, and Uncle Jack loved seeing the smile on his face. Gordon's little hands held the steering wheel tightly close to Uncle Jack's big hands. Gordon felt so proud to be helping his uncle plow the fields. Gordon thought about how he always rode in his dad's truck and sat on his dad's lap, steering the truck.

"I wish my mom and dad could see me driving this tractor, Uncle Jack. Thank you for letting me help you plow the cotton fields. My Momma would be proud of me, wouldn't she, Uncle Jack?"

"I'm proud of you, Gordon, and I want you helping me." Uncle Jack told him. Gordon placed his little hands on top of Uncle Jack's big hands, and they plowed until lunchtime.

When they returned to the house for lunch, Uncle Jack let Gordon turn the key and shut the tractor off. Then, Uncle Jack climbed down and grabbed Gordon to help him get off the red tractor. Gordon hugged Uncle Jack around his neck and kissed him, telling him how much he loved him. Gordon whispered in Uncle Jack's ear, "You are like a daddy now, Uncle Jack."

❦❧

Uncle Jack and Cornell finished breakfast and headed to the barn to fire up the red tractor. They had a lot of work to do today, and Uncle Jack was anxious to get a head start on his part of preparations for the Christmas Bazaar. He was happy Cornell had come to spend the weekend with him and Aunt Lottie.

When they reached the Community Barn, Uncle Jack parked the red tractor under a big old elm tree. Then he climbed off the tractor and watched Cornell jump down, yelling, "Geronimo!" Uncle Jack unloaded the tools from the tractor, and Cornell helped carry some into the barn."

Cornell walked around the spacious barn, investigating the place's nooks, crooks, and crannies. "Wow, Uncle Jack, I forgot how big this barn is," Cornell said, looking up towards the wooded beamed ceiling and twirling himself around. "We sure had fun building it, didn't we?"

"Yes, sir, we did, and now everyone enjoys all the celebrations, bazaars, and dances held here. The community has had many happy and wonderful times over the past two years." Uncle Jack told Cornell.

"What are we going to do today, Uncle Jack?" Cornell asked.

"We need to check the roof for damage and look for broken windows, any loose boards, and any other possible damage from the storm," Uncle Jack said. "We had better get busy so we can finish before lunchtime. I think I'm already hungry," Uncle Jack told Cornell. "Me, too," Cornell said, shaking his head up and down. Lolly packed us some snacks just in case we got hungry before lunch.

$\approx\!\cdot\!\ll$

Abby had several appointments with vendors in Gail. She called Aunt Lottie to let her know she wouldn't be home for lunch because she was having lunch with Mayor Stewart and his wife to discuss the menu for their 50th wedding anniversary celebration.

Lottie didn't usually have lunch alone, but it seemed she would today. Uncle Jack and Cornell hadn't shown up, and it was past lunchtime. She felt sure Cornell was probably out of snacks and that they would show up soon. But she was worried when they hadn't returned by two o'clock for lunch.

Lottie also became concerned about Grandpa Cliff and Old Shepp because she had not seen them since they walked Mollie down to her pasture. Lottie knew Grandpa Cliff checked on the other cows while there, but it didn't usually take him this long. Also, Old Shepp usually returns to the porch after a while and sleeps on his braided rug.

Lottie had been so busy working in the garden that she decided she needed a rest, so she went and sat down on the porch swing. After that, she decided to bake a pie and didn't realize how late it was until Abby called and said she would stay in Gail and have lunch with Mayor Stewart and his wife.

$\approx\!\cdot\!\ll$

Uncle Jack and Cornell finished most of the inspection of the Community Barn. They were thankful that the storm had not damaged the roof, but they did find a few windows broken when a tree limb broke off and hit a window in an upstairs office. They didn't find any water damage, so it is evident that the wind broke the limb off. It landed against the glass, cracking it; later, the wind pushed it through. Uncle Jack measured the glass and decided to check if he had some glass in the barn.

"Let's go and load up," Uncle Jack told Cornell. "I bet Aunt Lottie is waiting for us to eat lunch." Jack looked at his watch and was surprised it was past two o'clock. "Oh, my goodness, Cornell. We've missed lunch, and Aunt Lottie will not be happy with us."

Jack loaded the tools into the red tractor, helped Cornell climb into the seat, and climbed aboard. He turned the key, the red tractor started, and they headed home.

When they drove up, they saw Aunt Lottie sitting in her rocking chair on the porch. She waved to them as they passed, then put the red tractor in the barn. Grandpa Cliff liked to keep his red tractor parked in the barn.

Lottie walked over to welcome them home from a hard day's work. She told them she had a sandwich, iced tea, and apple pie waiting for them. "I can't believe you are this late coming home. What took you so long?" Aunt Lottie asked.

"We had no idea it was this late. I'm sorry," Jack answered, asking for forgiveness. "Can we still have some of that apple pie you said you had? Sure, sounds good, doesn't it, Cornell?" Uncle Jack commented, looking at Cornell. "Yes, sir." Cornell turned to Aunt Lottie and said, "I want some, please, Lolly."

Aunt Lottie got up and proceeded to the kitchen, with Cornell and Uncle Jack following behind. She fixed sandwiches for them, got Uncle Jack some iced tea and Cornell a glass of milk, and then sliced each a piece of apple pie.

"So, where's my dad?" Uncle Jack asked. "I didn't see Mollie in the barn, and Old Shepp is not asleep on his rug, and my dad is not asleep in his chair. Where are they?"

"I'm not sure," Lottie answered. "I was about to walk to the pasture when I heard you coming, so I waited. I haven't seen him since mid-morning after you left for the community barn. You know he checks on all the cows, but that doesn't usually take long. Also, he didn't show up for lunch, so I figured he may have gone with Doc Wilson, who stopped by to check on Mollie's leg." Aunt Lottie explained. "Usually, he tells me what he's doing or where he is going. Also, Old Shepp likes to stay down in the pasture if your dad is there, so I wasn't too concerned."

"Can I run to the pasture to see Mollie and see if Old Shepp and Grandpa Cliff are there?" Cornell asked.

"Sure, you go ahead, and I'll meet you down there as soon as I have another piece of pie," Uncle Jack said, giving Cornell a pat on the head and Aunt Lottie a big pleading smile. Uncle Jack was practically begging for another piece of pie.

Cornell opened the back door, ran, and jumped off the porch. He started skipping down the road towards Mollie's pasture. Cornell loved seeing Mollie and all the other cows and running through the pasture with Old Shepp. Sometimes, they would see a rabbit or two, and occasionally, Cornell would catch a glimpse of a deer in the heavily wooded area.

Lottie sat with Jack while he ate a second piece of pie and asked about the damage to the Community Barn. Jack gave her a full report and told her everything could be repaired within a week, which was a relief. All the events scheduled at the Community Barn could proceed as planned.

Cornell reached the gate and noticed it was halfway open. He didn't see Grandpa Cliff but noticed Mollie standing beside the gate. Old Shepp was lying down behind Mollie, so Cornell walked over to see if Old Shepp was hurt. That's when he saw Grandpa Cliff lying on the ground, and the rope attached to Mollie's harness was still in his hand.

He hurried over to him and tried to wake him. "Grandpa Cliff, wake up. Please wake up," he yelled, shaking him. But Grandpa Cliff didn't move.

Cornell was frightened and started crying and screaming for help while running back to the house to get Uncle Jack and Aunt Lottie to help Grandpa Cliff.

Uncle Jack and Aunt Lottie hurried towards Cornell and held him close. "It's okay, Cornell. Tell us what's wrong with Grandpa Cliff and where he is?" Uncle Jack asked, trying to calm him down.

"He's lying in the pasture, and Mollie is standing by the gate. The gate was open part way," Cornell answered between sobs. "I tried to wake him, but he wouldn't move. He needs help. I think he's hurt bad." Cornell tried to keep talking but began crying uncontrollably.

Uncle Jack and Aunt Lottie hurried to the pasture and found Grandpa Cliff lying where Cornell told them. Jack hurried, checked for a pulse, then he bent down and tried to resuscitate him. He put his ear to his dad's chest, but he still couldn't hear a heartbeat. Lottie bent down beside Jack, and they both knew Grandpa Cliff had died.

Jack looked at Lottie and said, "I think my dad died, Lottie. He was here with his two best friends, Mollie and Old Shepp, and he just died." Jack was highly emotional by now. "Look, he's still holding Mollie's rope in his hands. Oh, why wasn't I here for him?" Jack said while sobbing.

"Jack, we need to call Dr. Wilson," Lottie said while she rubbed Jack's shoulders to comfort him.

"Jack, you stay here, and I'll take Cornell back to the house with me and call.

Chapter Three

*T*he following days were extremely hard for the family as they arranged Grandpa Cliffs' funeral. On the funeral day, the entire family surrounded Lottie and Jack and respectfully said goodbye to their patriarch.

Standing beside his father's grave, Jack said, "My dad was Grandpa Cliff to our family and the many friends here today. There are no words to relate what he truly meant to all of us. He was a pillar of strength in bad times, an encourager when decisions were made, and a beam of light to guide you when you had lost your way. I know he will be greatly missed. We loved him so very, very much. Lottie and I thank you all for being here today."

For the first time in Jack's life, his dad wouldn't be there to encourage him, advise him about what he should do, or sit on the porch and share a glass of iced tea. He wouldn't be there to walk Mollie down to the pasture or watch Old Shepp chase a rabbit behind the barn. He wouldn't be there to share another Christmas, ride the red tractor, or meet his newest great-grandchild. Grandpa Cliff would no longer be among them, but his life would be forever etched on their hearts.

Lottie knew Grandpa Cliff had come to the graveyard for the last time. His body would now reside in the ground next to his beloved Hannah and firstborn son, Jeffery. He would no longer visit the cemetery or be concerned about the red tractor. Sometimes, there is comfort in facing the final journey of the life of your loved one.

Jack always had his dad's help with harvesting the cotton. Life would be quite different now, but Lottie and Jack adjusted with the encouragement of family and friends. Josh even attended the funeral and offered to assist Jack with harvesting the cotton crop.

After the funeral, everyone gathered at the Community Center Barn for a potluck dinner and enjoyed a time of fellowship and sharing remembrances of Grandpa Cliff and his wife, Hannah, and offered Lottie and Jack their support in the days ahead.

Abby was busy keeping an eye on Cornell and watching over Emily Jean. Although the occasion was sad, Abby enjoyed the family being together again so soon after Aunt Lottie's birthday. She felt happy that Grandpa Cliff enjoyed the birthday party with his best friend, Alma, who was his date at the party. No one expected him to be gone so soon after.

Josh saw Abby across the room, talking with Mayor Stewart and Lizzie. As soon as they walked away, Josh approached Abby and put his arm around her shoulders. "Abby, I am so sorry for your loss. Grandpa Cliff was a man I greatly respected."

"Thanks, Josh. I appreciate you being here," Abby replied with a tear in her eye. "He was a very good and loving man. I wish you could have known him. I wish I would have taken the time to visit more often." Abby began to tear up. She began to realize how much she missed being in New York. "You know, he was there when I watched my mother die. When I held her hand in mine, he stayed near me when they found me and Gordon on the muddy road in the cotton field. He told me that there wasn't anything we could have done to save her. He and Uncle Jack rescued us when the car overturned and trapped my mother underneath. We were alone in the cotton field, and it was so dark, and we were so scared. We didn't know what to do. Nobody could hear us crying and screaming for help."

Abby couldn't believe she was telling Josh all of this. Her heart was heavy, and she realized the sacrifices she had made. She thought she was following a dream and would find success in New York while working in a large and prestigious firm. Now, she realized she had success at her fingertips, being with a loving family who had loved her and given her a life of love. The greatest thing she missed was her family and friends.

Josh took her hand and asked her to walk outside with him. The full moon shone beautifully across the cotton fields. They walked hand in hand to a bench and sat silently for a short while.

"Abby, in life, you can't walk backward," Josh told her as he looked deeply into her eyes. "You move forward. Love never dies in the heart of someone who loves you. No matter what you choose yesterday, today is what you have." Abby looked into Josh's eyes and gave him a look of appreciation. She was taken by what he said and began to think about her feelings for him. She realized the hole in her heart was not the time spent in New York. It wasn't just birthdays, the holidays, the time spent with family. She realized now that the hole in her heart was the absence of Josh in her life.

Abby leaned over to Josh, kissed him on the cheek, then rested her head on his shoulder. She felt her love for Josh flowing through her heart again.

Chapter Four

*I*t was a long, lonely walk taking Mollie to the pasture. Uncle Jack walked a little slower; Mollie acted somewhat differently, as if to say, 'Where's Grandpa Cliff?' Old Shepp tagged slowly behind. Everything seemed out of place. Jack had never lived without his dad nearby. When Jack and Lottie married, Jack's parents enlarged their house so they could all live on the cotton farm together. After all, that's all his parents had ever known and all he had ever known. Now, Jack would have to navigate life as the family patriarch and do his best to follow in his father's footsteps. Jack was the sole heir to his father's estate: possessions and responsibilities.

Uncle Jack returned to the barn and climbed into the red tractor. He just wanted to be there and think about how life can change in a heartbeat. Just a few days ago, his dad was working on the red tractor, and today, the red tractor, his dad's prized possession, was sitting in the barn and would never be driven by his dad again. Jack needed time to pull himself together before returning to the house and having breakfast with Lottie and Abby. He would be later than usual, but he knew Lottie would understand.

As Jack walked up on the porch, he couldn't help but notice the empty chair where his dad usually sat and drank his morning coffee. Even Old Shepp wasn't on his rug, as usual. He had entered the house and laid on the braided rug in the living room.

Jack hesitated before entering the house. He stood on the porch for a while, looking over the cotton fields. It was close to harvest time; this would be his first harvest without his dad. He sighed, took a deep breath, and walked to the kitchen.

Lottie walked over and gave him a hug and a kiss. Uncle Jack asked about Abby's whereabouts, and Aunt Lottie told him she had already left. They would quietly have breakfast together.

❧❧

When Abby arrived at her office, she found a large package and a stack of mail on her desk. A sticky note on the top of the package read, "Abby, I think these are the invitations you ordered. Mayor Stewart."

Abby anxiously opened the package, and sure enough, the mayor was correct. She called him, told him they were the invitations, and asked if he and Lizzie had the guest list complete. She was anxious to start addressing them since the event was only three weeks away. She planned for people to receive their invitations two weeks before the event, giving them time to RSVP. Abby opened the invitations to be sure all the information was correct. As she read over them, she felt a twinge of sadness because Grandpa Cliff would not be there, and Alma, his lifelong friend, would not have an escort for the occasion. Alma had mentioned to Abby how much she missed Grandpa Cliff and always looked forward to going places with him. They had a deep friendship, not a romantic one.

Alma and Grandpa Cliff were high school classmates. Alma introduced him to Hannah, her best friend, who didn't have a date for the Senior Prom. When Cliff met Hannah, it was love at first sight. Cliff and Hannah dated for six months and married in November after the cotton harvest. Their hearts were entwined, and their goals in life were conducive to their plans. Hannah's family owned and managed the local cotton gin, and Cliff's family owned one of the largest cotton farms west of Synder, Texas.

Mayor Stewart called his wife, Lizzie, about the guest list and instructed her to bring it to his office or Abby's as soon as possible. He was looking forward to this celebration with great anticipation. And since it was going to be held in the very place where they were married, he felt it would be like their wedding was happening all over again.

❧❦

Abby heard a knock on her office door, and thinking it was Mrs. Stewart bringing the guest list to her, she politely said, "Come in." What a surprise it was when Josh walked in with a big smile.

"I hope I'm not interrupting your work schedule?" Josh politely said. "I tried calling you to see if you would have lunch with me today, but there was no answer."

"I'm sorry, Josh, I never heard my phone ring," Abby replied apologetically. "Where is that thing anyway," she mumbled.

"Would you be able to leave for lunch, or should I go and pick up some barbecue from Smitty's? That's just down the road," Josh asked, hoping for a positive answer.

"That sounds wonderful, Josh," Abby replied as she shut her desk drawer and locked it. "Let's go. I love good ole Texas barbecue."

Riding to Smitty's with Josh felt like stepping into a different world. It had been ages since she could decide where and when to have lunch. She was free to live again. She was comfortable in Josh's presence and looked forward to spending more time with him.

"Abby, I don't know what Uncle Jack's plans are for harvesting his cotton crop, but I want you to know that I am more than willing to help him. I know he has probably done this alone before, but if he needs help, I want to be there for him."

"There hasn't been much time to think about it yet, but I will be sure to let him know about your offer," Abby replied. "I know very little about harvesting cotton. I can drive the red tractor, but I know nothing about those huge machines. "Oh, while I'm thinking about it," Abby continued, "I look forward to coming to your birthday party. I've never been to Sugarland Ranch. Is that new?"

"Yes, and no. They turned the old skating facility into a dancing club with food, drinks, and visiting bands. The skating area is now a dance floor," Josh informed Abby. I will gladly come and get you the night of the party. I was going to ask you to come personally, but my mom said she had already sent you an invitation." Josh felt good about Abby's plan to be at his party.

Abby and Josh enjoyed a relaxing lunch at Smitty's. Josh was proud to introduce Abby to several of his close friends there, whom he often met for lunch. So much had changed in their circle of friends since Abby left for New York almost eight years ago. It was becoming evident to Abby that Josh had never given up on hoping for a relationship with her again.

Abby and Josh's relationship grew more profoundly over the next few weeks. Josh was often at the farm, helping Uncle Jack with the harvest. Many evenings, Josh was encouraged to stay and eat dinner with Aunt Lottie, Uncle Jack, and Abby. It wasn't unusual for Abby to walk with Josh out to his truck, and Aunt Lottie would often see Josh hug Abby and kiss her goodnight from the kitchen window. Aunt Lottie would smile to herself, and she could see their love developing into something more than renewed friendship. Aunt Lottie felt Josh and Abby were creating a serious relationship.

☙❧

Over the last couple of weeks, Aunt Lottie and Uncle Jack experienced many challenges since Grandpa Cliff's death. Life continues to change drastically, and it is hard to navigate the void his death has brought to their lives, from having coffee in the morning to walking Mollie back to the barn at night. It is different, not only for them but for everyone who has known Grandpa Cliff.

Chapter Five

*A*bby was in a dilemma. She had a lot of clothes but wanted something new for Josh's birthday party—something more fitting for a Texas lassie than a New York Executive. The parties that Abby had planned and attended were very sophisticated. What she had in her wardrobe needed change. She had nice jeans, shirts, and blouses but no casual dresses or skirts. She wanted something with a fresh and soft look. Also, she didn't have a pair of dressy western boots.

"Aunt Lottie, would you go shopping with me in Sweetwater? I need some clothes to wear to casual events here in Gail. Also, Josh is having a birthday party, and I have nothing to wear except jeans and shirts. So much of my wardrobe is mainly jeans, blouses, workout clothes, classy dresses, and pantsuits. I don't feel any of it will work." Abby said, sounding pathetic.

"Sure. When are you planning to go?" Aunt Lottie asked. "Sounds like we could have a lady's day out! It's been ages since I've been to Sweetwater, or just shopping, for that matter. I hear several new classy shops have just opened up in the past month or so

"Would you be able to go tomorrow if we left early and got back in time to fix dinner for Uncle Jack?" Abby answered. "My friend from college who lives in Abilene says she shops there and finds the most amazing things at this unique shop that her cousin manages. Also, she knows of an excellent boot shop specializing in unique designs.

"Let me talk with Uncle Jack later, and I'll tell you for sure. Sounds like fun." Aunt Lottie told her.

❧❧

When Abby saw the Stewart's guest list, it was like journeying into the past. There were so many names of people she knew from when she lived with Aunt Lottie and Uncle Jack. She was surprised that she could recall association with many of the mayor's friends.

Abby attended school in Gail from 3rd grade until she graduated High School. Gordon started Kindergarten in Gail and went there until he graduated High School. It was surprising to see how many teachers who had moved out of Texas were still in touch with Mayor Stewart. This was not only going to be an anniversary celebration, but it was also going to be a homecoming for so many, including Gordon and Abby.

Abby worked diligently to get all the anniversary party invitations mailed on time. She couldn't believe the date was so close and knew she needed to receive replies shortly, either confirming or declining to attend.

Mayor Stewart called Abby to see if the decorations had arrived since Lizzie asked to see them. She also told Abby the number of confirmations they had received from those who planned to attend. The numbers were increasing, and Abby was anxious to get a final guest count to confirm with the caterers.

When Lizzie saw the decorations, she told Abby she was pleased because they looked exactly like the ones in her wedding pictures. Abby felt a sense of nostalgia looking at them. The parlor and the ballroom would look like they did 50 years ago. Abby hoped this would be a journey into the past for Mayor Stewart and Lizzie.

❦

The shopping trip to Sweetwater was a success. Abby and Aunt Lottie left early and got to Sweetwater by eleven o'clock. They went to the little café Abby's friend recommended for brunch and then started shopping. Every store they visited was a fantastic experience, and Abby was overjoyed to share Aunt Lottie's excitement with her.

Abby found the perfect dress to wear to Josh's party and a pair of gorgeous western boots that were an ideal complement to her outfit for the evening. She was comfortable with her choices.

Aunt Lottie found a dress for the mayor's anniversary party. She hadn't bought a new dress in such a long time, and Abby encouraged her to buy one. They found the perfect dress made of bridle taffeta with a sheer chiffon overlay in the most beautiful lavender color. The bodice was covered in scattered pearls--- a dress fit for a queen. Lavender was the perfect color for Aunt Lottie because it highlighted her silver-toned hair and hazel eyes. And the shoes Aunt Lottie found were just like the ones she wore at her wedding, only silver instead of white.

"Wait until Uncle Jack sees you all dressed up for the party! He will be unable to take his eyes off you because you are his beautiful lady, Aunt Lottie." Abby said, admiring her. "Gosh, I love you, and I'm so glad we spent the day together." Abby hugged her, then said. "Let's do it again."

૎૏

Large clay pots of poinsettias wrapped with white satin ribbon and a large bow lined the steps leading to the entryway of the exquisite Victorian house where Mayor Stewart and his wife, Lizzie, were hosting their 50th Wedding Anniversary Party. Everyone who entered marveled at the architectural beauty of such an old house. The house belonged to Mayor Stewart's grandparents, who purchased it in 1888. Mayor Stewart and Lizzie considered it an honor to have been married in that house 50 years ago.

૎૏

"Abby, you look so beautiful tonight," Josh said, looking into her eyes.

"Thank you, Josh. I'm so glad you came. I was hoping you would be here early so I could show you around," Abby told him as she took his hand and began walking through the house with him.

"Wow! This is a beautiful house," Josh told Abby as they walked past the wooden circular stairway to the second floor. "The decorations are stunning," Josh continued to comment to Abby. "You know how to decorate for an event."

As they walked into the ballroom, Josh looked around the vast room and at the wooden beams on the ceiling from which crystal lights hung. "When did you say this house was built?" Josh asked.

"It was built in 1882 by a family who owned acres and acres of cotton fields." Abby began to relate the history of the house to Josh. Then, as their family increased, they sold this house to Mayor Stewart's grandparents, who raised their children in it. When his grandmother passed away, Mayor Stewart became the sole heir to the house."

"It's so interesting to hear the history of old houses and buildings here in our part of Texas," Josh commented. "Most of the time, buildings are torn down to build new ones rather than restoring the old ones. I appreciate that about our part of the country, don't you?"

Abby answered, "Yes, of course. I like the history behind our area's many buildings, homes, and barns. When Mayor Stewart inherited the house, he restored it but kept it as original as possible. He kept all the windows, especially the beautiful stained-glass windows in the parlor. He also restored the ornate wooden staircase and moldings. And best of all, he had the fountain in the Garden Room repaired, which is such a soothing and comforting place to sit and admire its beauty".

"Josh, please excuse me for a moment. I need to check on the caterers; I think the band has arrived. They need to know where to set up their equipment," Abby said. Also, I've got to direct Mayor Stewart and Lizzie to where they need to stand to greet their guests when they arrive. I'll be back shortly."

Josh watched as Abby walked away to check on the caterers, direct the band to their set-up location, and find the mayor and his wife. The more he observed Abby, the more he became assured of his love for her. He couldn't stop watching her every move.

Aunt Lottie and Uncle Jack arrived, and after being greeted by Mayor Stewart and Lizzie, they looked around to find Abby. As they were looking for her, they saw Josh and walked over to him to say hello. "Josh, we're so glad you could be here today. Have you seen Abby?" Uncle Jack asked, still looking for her.

"Yes, sir," Josh answered. "She's in the ballroom showing the band where to set up."

Uncle Jack and Aunt Lottie went to the ballroom and found Abby giving the band instructions on where to set up. When Abby saw them, she hurried over to greet them and told them that Josh had come.

"We know, we already saw him," Uncle Jack told her. "Josh sure looks handsome tonight, doesn't he?" Abby smiled and nodded yes.

"And, wow, look at you," Uncle Jack said, looking at Abby. "You are so beautiful tonight, and that's a beautiful dress."

Uncle Jack leaned over to Abby and whispered, "Doesn't Aunt Lottie look gorgeous? You gals sure did good on your shopping trip to Sweetwater."

Abby just beamed. She hugged them both and said she needed to look for Josh since she had left him alone when she needed to tend to business.

❧❦

The celebration was off to a good start. After mingling among their guests, the mayor and his wife were seated at their table. The buffet was served to guests, and the band played soft music.

Josh, Abby, Aunt Lottie, and Uncle Jack sat at a table together, enjoying the evening's ambiance. Josh recognized the song being played, and it brought back a deep emotional memory of his days in college when he and Abby had what he thought was a serious relationship. The song playing was the same song he and Abby first danced together at a fraternity party, and he fell in love with her. At that moment, he knew he wanted Abby in his life forever. He never thought Abby would leave West Texas to follow what she felt was her future and take a job in New York. But here Josh was again, with Abby and the song being played. He stood up, put his hand out toward her, and asked, "Abby, would you dance with me?"

Abby got up, offered her hand to Josh, and together, they walked to the center of the dance floor. They danced to the treasured song in Josh's memory and Abby's memory of their shared past relationship. While they danced, Josh whispered into Abby's ear, saying, "How wonderful it is to hold you in my arms again. Through all the years spent apart, me living and working here in Texas and you in New York, my love for you never died. I had always hoped that someday you would return to West Texas, and we would be together again." Abby never took her eyes off Josh and was touched by his words.

❧❦

Abby remembered her disappointments in New York but was too proud to leave her position in the firm where she worked and admit to them. She didn't want to feel like a failure by leaving her job. She didn't want to face the fact that she had made a mistake by leaving a life she was comfortable living to adjust to one that made her uncomfortable. She felt she would embarrass her family, and she wanted to make her family proud. Being offered the prestigious job in New York gave her the satisfaction of making them proud. She never realized her family was already proud of her achievements by being a young woman who survived a profound emotional tragedy. Abby was only seven years old when she lay next to her mother on a muddy road amid the cotton fields, holding her mother's hand after she tried to pull her out from underneath their overturned car. She watched her mother take her last breath and felt responsible for not being able to save her.

Abby took the job in New York with the hope of erasing the memory of her mother's death, which was never going to happen. The memory would always be there because it was part of her life. Only because of Aunt Lottie and Uncle Jack did she find the love and courage to walk forward.

Josh felt a deep emptiness when Abby left West Texas and went to live and work in New York. He was grateful when his best friend from college needed help managing his mother and father's cotton farm in Floyd County. Josh jumped at the opportunity and spent several years working there, which helped to fill the void that Abby left in his life. Even though Josh visited Abby while she lived in New York, she wasn't the Abby Josh knew and loved in Texas. Corporate life had changed her, and even though Abby begged him to come live in New York, Josh knew that could never work out.

❦❧

When the music stopped, Josh asked Abby if she would like a drink and if she would like to go to the garden room to sit and talk. The room was beautifully decorated with miniature fir trees adorned in white lights that illuminated the room and created a magical appearance. At the far end of the room was a fountain with a beautiful angel statue standing in the middle, its hands extended towards the statues of a little boy and a little girl leaning over and looking into the pool of water to see their reflection. Water entered the fountain from jets under the angel's feet, creating a soothing sound as the water flowed over a rock bed and reflected the room's lights.

Josh chose a table where they could sit and enjoy the view of the entire room, especially the fountain. They could hear the band playing, but Josh was more interested in sitting and talking with Abby. Josh's heart was filled with love for Abby, and he was trying to find a way to tell her that his love for her had never died and he still wanted to spend the rest of his life with her.

"Josh, isn't this just a beautiful place? Abby said, opening the conversation. "I am so happy that you came tonight. You have made this evening special for me."

Josh moved his chair closer to Abby's and put his arm around her shoulders. He just wanted to be as close to her as he could.

"This is a great room for a wedding," Josh commented, looking at the beauty of the room and Abby's beauty in the glow of the lanterns that hung from the ceiling,

Abby looked into Josh's eyes, smiled, and asked him, "Do you know anyone getting married?"

Josh pulled her closer and whispered, "Hopefully, we will."

The End

KNOW THE AUTHOR

The years have a way of swiftly transitioning from childhood to adulthood, each moment weaving the tapestry of our lives. My journey began with the cherished mornings spent with my father, riding in his truck to the coal mines. My father was a coal retailer, and growing up in St. Louis, his business taught me invaluable lessons about resilience and the warmth people seek during the harshest winters. Those early years taught me practical skills—driving on snow, building snowmen and snow forts, ice skating, and piloting a sled down a steep, snowy hill. These memories, steeped in nostalgia, form the foundation of my storytelling.

Reading was not just a pastime for me; it was a lifeline, a portal to different parts of the United States and beyond. Through books, I journeyed with characters, entering their lives and living their experiences. Reading is not merely words on a page; it's a journey with the book's characters, and you become part of their world. This immersion into different worlds and experiences fueled my love for writing, allowing me to share my life's stories, thoughts, and knowledge.

Years ago, someone asked me how I knew what to write in a book. My answer was simple: "When I am inspired by the thought or action of someone or something, I write that 'something' down in words, and that 'something' becomes' SOMETHING. ' Inspiration is the seed from which stories grow, and I find inspiration in everyday life, transforming the ordinary into the extraordinary through my writing.

In this book, we travel with Abby as she renews her love for the life she knew as a child. Her journey of self-discovery and rekindling old passions mirrors my experiences of finding joy and purpose in the simplest moments.

I invite you to dive into the entire Cottonfield Sunset series and follow Abby's captivating journey of love and self-discovery. In the third book, her quest to embrace life continues, filled with secrets and answers waiting to be uncovered. Join me in exploring Abby's inspiring story—a testament to the enduring human spirit.